What Firefighters Do?

Written by Tracey Michele

Picture Dictionary

burning buildings

forest fires

car accidents

school visits

chemical spills

Firefighters do a lot of jobs.
They have to keep fit
to do their jobs.

These firefighters are doing
push-ups to keep fit.

Firefighters wear special clothes
to keep safe.
They have special tools, too.

Firefighters' Tools

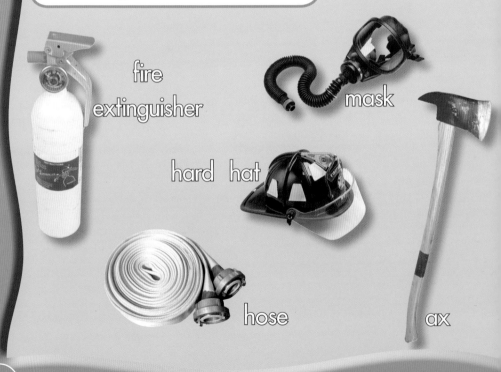

fire
extinguisher

mask

hard hat

hose

ax

hard hat

jacket

glove

pants

boot

This firefighter has fireproof clothes.

Burning Buildings

Firefighters put out fires
in buildings.
Some fires are near the top
of buildings.
Firefighters have to climb ladders
to put out these fires.

oxygen tank

This firefighter is at the top of an extension ladder.

Forest Fires

Firefighters put out forest fires.
They clear a strip of land.
This is called a firebreak.
Forest fires cannot go
over firebreaks.
Firefighters drop water
on forest fires, too.

bucket

This helicopter is dropping water on a forest fire.

Car Accidents

Firefighters help at accidents.
They put out fires in cars.
They cut the car up
to get out the people
who are inside.

safety glove

These firefighters are cutting up this car.

Chemical Spills

Firefighters help
when chemicals are spilled.
They use foam to put out fires.
They clean up chemicals
that have spilled on the ground.

special coveralls

Firefighters need special clothes for chemical spills.

School Visits

Firefighters go to schools.
They tell children about fires.
They tell children what to do
if there is a fire.
They tell children not to play
with matches.

fire truck

This firefighter is talking to some children.

Activity Page

1. Draw a picture of a firefighter doing one of their many jobs.

2. Write two sentences about your picture.

Do you know the dictionary words?